For my angel. GS
For Sheila, how I wish you were here. PS
For Sheila Barry, with gratitude ... MP

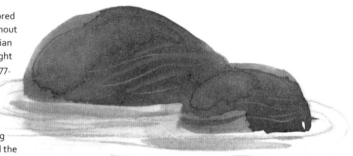

Text copyright © 2019 by Patricia Elaine Storms and Guy Lawrence Storms
Illustrations copyright © 2019 by Milan Pavlović
Published in Canada and the USA in 2019 by Groundwood Books

Groundwood Books / House of Anansi Press
groundwoodbooks.com

We gratefully acknowledge for their financial support of our publishing
program the Canada Council for the Arts, the Ontario Arts Council and the
Government of Canada.

Canada Council   Conseil des Arts
for the Arts   du Canada

ONTARIO ARTS COUNCIL
CONSEIL DES ARTS DE L'ONTARIO
an Ontario government agency
un organisme du gouvernement de l'Ontario

With the participation of the Government of Canada   Canada
Avec la participation du gouvernement du Canada

Library and Archives Canada Cataloguing in Publication
Storms, Patricia, author
Moon wishes / Patricia Storms, Guy Storms ; [illustrated by] Milan Pavlović.
Issued in print and electronic formats.
ISBN 978-1-77306-076-7 (hardcover). — ISBN 978-1-77306-077-4 (PDF)
I. Storms, Guy, author II. Pavlović, Milan, illustrator III. Title.
PS8637.T6755M66 2019   jC813'.6   C2018-903523-4
C2018-903524-2

The illustrations were done in mixed media, drawing inks and color pencils.
Design by Michael Solomon
Printed and bound in Malaysia

FSC
www.fsc.org
MIX
Paper from
responsible sources
FSC® C012700

MOON WISHES

by

GUY AND PATRICIA STORMS

pictures by

MILAN PAVLOVIĆ

GROUNDWOOD BOOKS
HOUSE OF ANANSI PRESS
TORONTO   BERKELEY

If I were the moon, I would paint ripples of light on wet canvas and shimmer over dreams of snow.

I would wax and wane over the Earth's troubles,

wishing peaceful sleep for worried hearts.

If I were the moon, I would give a voice
to those who need it

and welcome the dark and joyful howls
of a winter night.

I would be a beacon for
the lost and lonely,

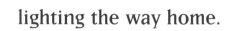
lighting the way home.

I wish I were the moon,
for the moon is a guide to
winged creatures.

If I were the moon,
I would light a
path for traveling
friends.

And if I were the moon, I would make myself
big and bright and strong with love

so that I could shine on you.

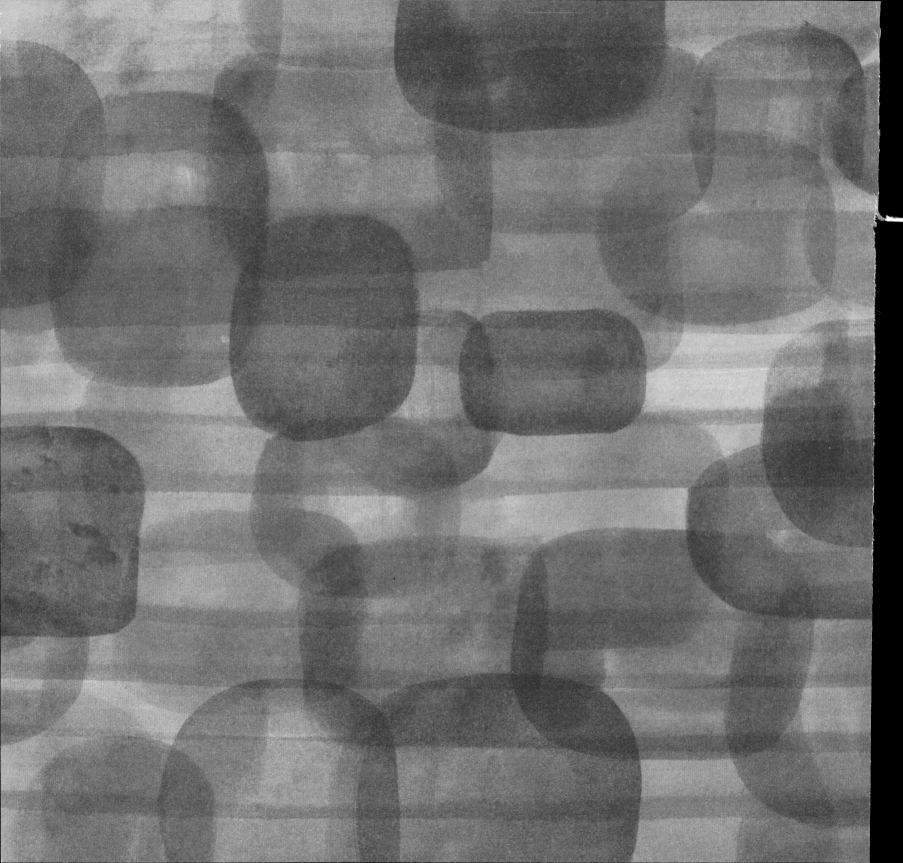